ALFIE

For Raquel, Maria and Llanos x P.M.

For the original Alfie McPoonst, the best dog ever. With all my love forever x D.McN.

First American Edition 2020
Kane Miller, A Division of EDC Publishing

Published by arrangement with Walker Books Ltd, 87 Vauxhall Walk, London SE11 5HJ

For information contact:
Kane Miller, A Division of EDC Publishing
P.O. Box 470663,
Tulsa, OK 74147-0663
www.kanemiller.com
www.usbornebooksandmore.com

Library of Congress Control Number: 2019940416

Printed in China
ISBN: 978-1-68464-027-0
1 2 3 4 5 6 7 8 9 10

Love From Alfie McPoonst

The Best Dog Ever

Dawn McNiff

illustrated by **Patricia Metola**

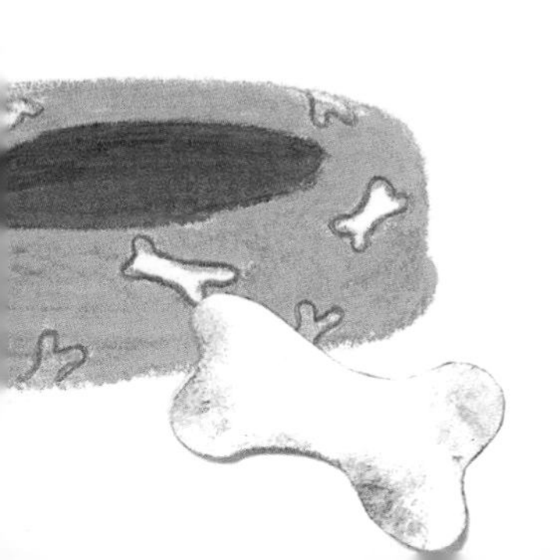

To Izzy
The Dog Bed
The Family Room
Izzy's House
Near the Little Park

Dear Izzy,

I'm a Sky Dog now.
I live in Dog Heaven,
because I died.

I miss you lots, but it's BRILLIANT here. There are hundreds of parks, thousands of sticks, and a million-trillion dog treats.

No cats bully me. I get to scare big wolves and chase postmen. I never need to have a bath. (There are no poodle parlors in Dog Heaven.) And the big dogs LOVE my good-boy-shake-a-paw trick!

Love from,
Alfie McPoonst x

PS I still miss you loads though.

Dear Izzy,
I get ALL my favorite meals here.
There are actual burger stands and ice cream trucks for dogs. And I'm allowed to eat cow pies.
Love from,
AMcPx

Dear Izzy,

Did I tell you I've got loads of Sky Dog friends?

We play tug-of-war with our teddies.
We go for walks by ourselves – nude,
without our collars or leads! We do roly-polies
in flower beds, squash all the flowers and
NO ONE shouts.

And we're allowed to snooze on sofas,
chew shoes, pee up slides and poop on lawns.
It's so fun.

Love from,
AMcPx

Dear Izzy,

I miss our huggles and tummy tickles.

But the BEST part of Heaven is that I get to snuggle with my dog mom again at bedtime.

Love from,

AMcPx

Dear Izzy,

I watch you through a star peephole every day. It makes my tail very waggy. Please wave.

Love from,

AMcPx

PS I left some dog fluff behind the sofa.

Alfie McPoonst
The Best Dog Ever
The Nicest Cloud
Dog Heaven
The Sky

Dear Alfie,

Thank you for my fluff.
I keep it in a special heart
locket, so I'll never forget
you, even when I'm 100.

Love from,
Izzy xx

PS I love you forever.